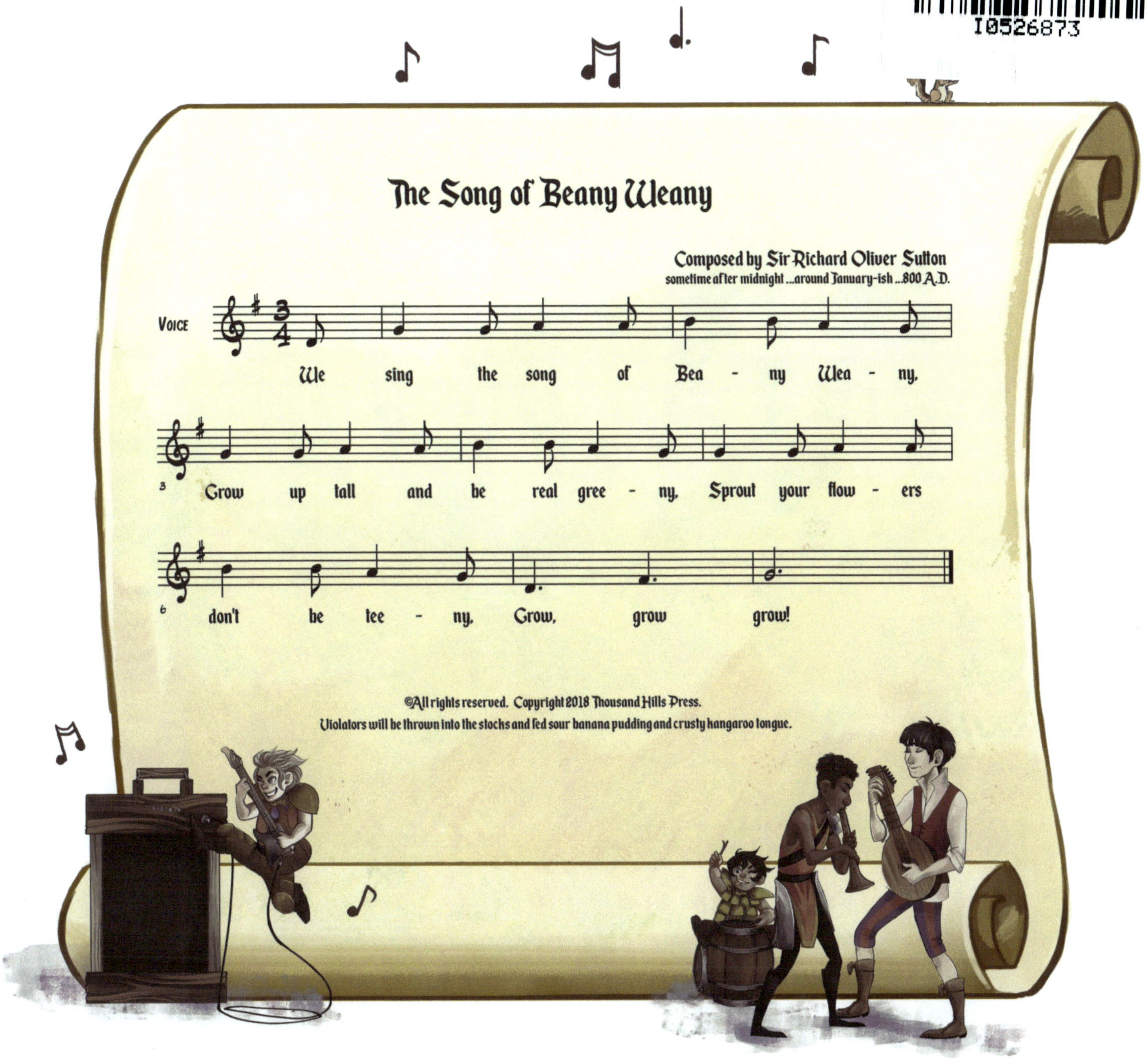
The Song of Beany Weany
Composed by Sir Richard Oliver Sutton
sometime after midnight ...around January-ish ...800 A.D.
Voice
We sing the song of Bea - ny Wea - ny.
3 Grow up tall and be real gree - ny. Sprout your flow - ers
6 don't be tee - ny. Grow, grow grow!
©All rights reserved. Copyright 2018 Thousand Hills Press.
Violators will be thrown into the stocks and fed sour banana pudding and crusty kangaroo tongue.

The Noble Knights of
Beany Weany

This book is in honor of The Porterboy Knights-
Dawson, Brayden, and Hudson. Hear ye!
Long live the adventurous tales of our bedtime imaginations
and may contagious giggles and delightful outburts never be forgotten.

I know we never will. :) Love you dearly
- Mom and Dad.

Printed in the United States of America
First Printing, 2018

ISBN: 173264490X
ISBN-13: 9781732644908

Thousand Hills Publishing
Grand Rapids, Michigan
www.kingdomofeverjoy.com

Publishing assistance provided by
Publish Pros | publishpros.com

The Noble Knights of
Beany Weany

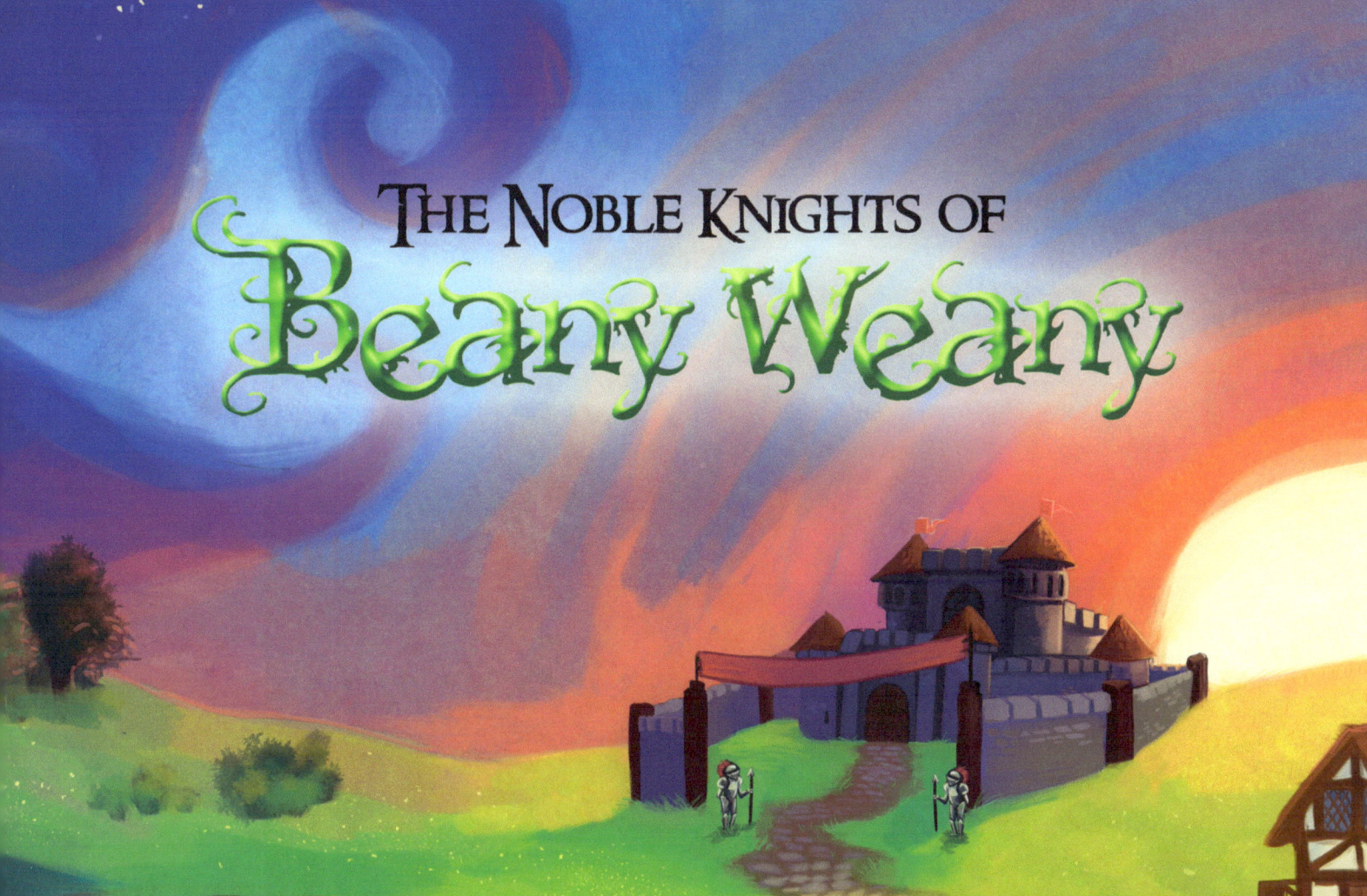

BRANT W. PORTER

Illustrated by Alyson Hüber

There once was a tale of three young boys
who lived in the Kingdom of Everjoy.
Although they were different in many ways,
their hearts were true and guided their days.

They awoke one morn to a rap at the door.
"King DaddiDoo needs **help**!"
"Oh no! What for?"

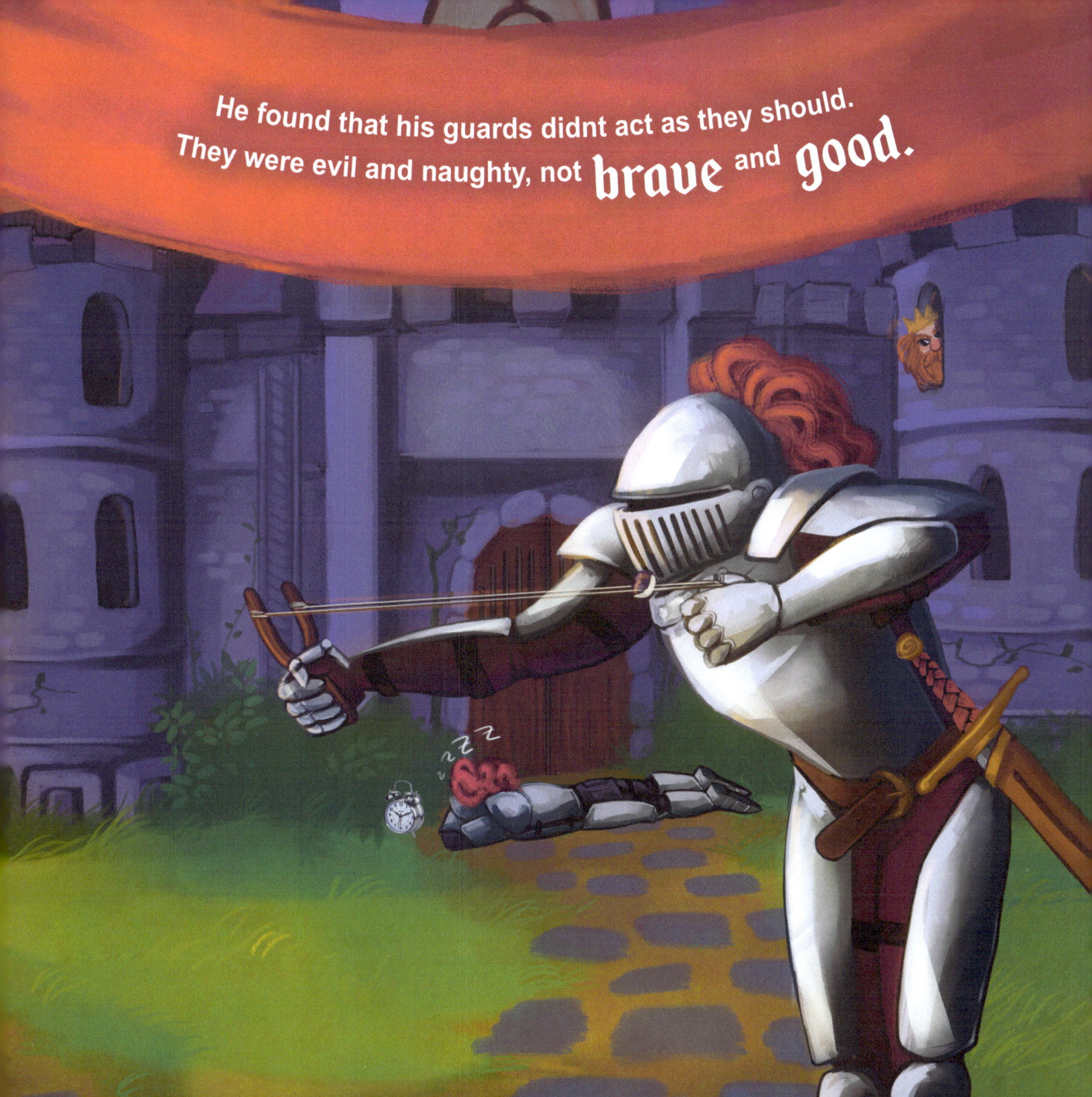

He found that his guards didnt act as they should.
They were evil and naughty, not **brave** and **good.**

So he held a contest
to fill their spots.
"Come grow the seeds
that are in these pots.
Whoever grows the most
wonderful tree
will gain great reward and
rule here with me."

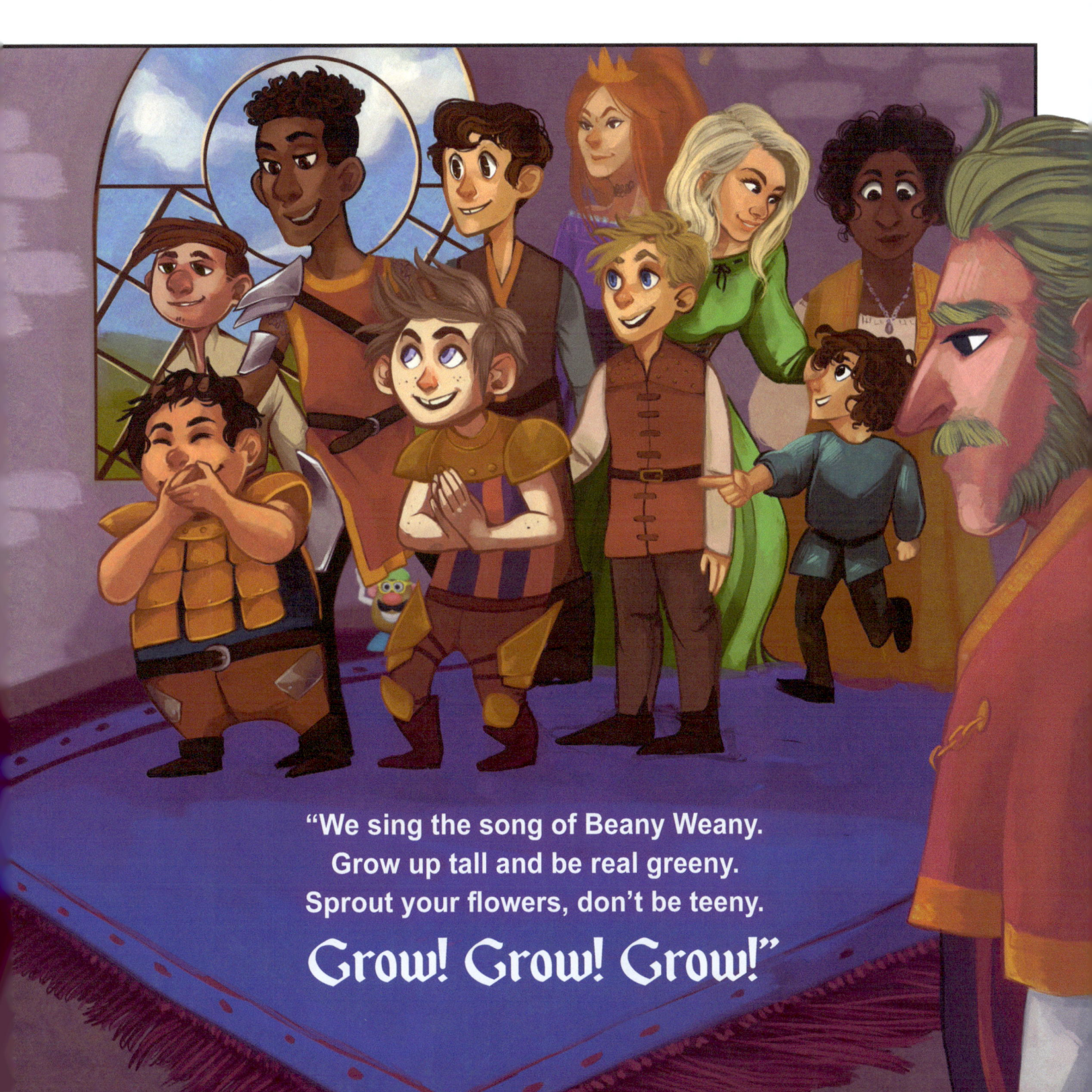

"We sing the song of Beany Weany.
Grow up tall and be real greeny.
Sprout your flowers, don't be teeny.
Grow! Grow! Grow!"

The Grumblies arrived. And Stinkypoos too.
A "not for real" princess, Ms. Betterthanyu.
The three young dudes came humble, yet strong.
They all took their pots and said "Game on!"

With water,
the sun and

encouragement,

their little seeds got
some nourishment.

Two weeks went by and nothing yet.
"Whatsa matter wit you! We're gonna
lose this bet."

"We sing the song of Beany Weany.
Grow up tall and be real greeny.
Sprout your flowers, don't be teeny.
Grow! Grow! Grow!"

Three months - it came,
and not a spud.
Then six months. Eight months.

"We've got a dud."

The day was near
when the king would call
and when he did,
the boys felt small.

"We **failed**. We're lame. Should we give up?
They'll laugh, they'll point and show us up."

But they grabbed their pot
and as they entered in, prayed "God,
please give us, a miracle... to win."

"We sing the song of Beany Weany.
Grow up tall and be real greeny.
Sprout your flowers, don't be teeny.
Grow! Grow! Grow!"

With trumpets' sound, King DaddiDoo came.
And walked, and strode amongst the game.
"Such beautiful trees and plants amidst.
The colors and growth - how splendid is this!"

He held his breath to announce the decree
of whom he'd chose:
the "Best of All" tree.

With the grandest of flair, in everyone's sight,
"These boys are the ones! YOU are my **knights**."

The crowd was **stunned.**

But then he explained
why he chose whom he did.
He held out some seeds
and here's what he said:

"The seeds I gave were already done.
Completely dead, no fruit would come.
You switched your seeds when nothing came.
You lied. You fakes. You stand in shame!"

But these daring three went against the grain.
They followed not, nor sought their fame.

With **integrity,** courage, and stout brave hearts,
they did what's good. They did what's smart!"

So here's the moral we all should learn:
It doesn't matter what others may spurn.

Plant what's right and
honor will grow.

and sing this song we've all come to know...

"We sing the song of Beany Weany.
Grow up tall and be real greeny.
Sprout your flowers, don't be teeny.

Grow! ...Grow! ...Grow!"

GO ONLINE FOR MORE OF THE ADVENTURE!

Can you find Sir Henry the Squirrel on every page? Or discover over 30+ secret items the Jester has hidden throughout the book!

Get the inside scoop on how it began!

Crazy fun facts and facebook profiles on all the characters!

Sing along with the audiobook of "Beany Weany" in hilarious different song styles!

Videos, puzzles, ...secrets,

AND SO MUCH MORE!

WWW.KINGDOMOFEVERJOY.COM

www.ingramcontent.com/pod-product-compliance
Lightning Source LLC
Chambersburg PA
CBHW041002170626
46815CB00002B/120